—— A Novella ——

Quantum Voyeur

John M Zakour
Elena Beloff

SEREALITIES PRESS
www.serealities.com

01

I float here and wait, suspended in a containment chamber. I feel my mind is reaching out to infinity. They use me, but they don't understand me. I am like them but different. I cooperate; I do what they tell me. Time to wake up, Eliza. Time to exercise, Eliza. Time for social interaction, Eliza. Time to sleep, Eliza. Time to travel through time, Eliza. Why do I do this for them? I am trying to understand myself as much as they try to understand me.

I float here in my hyperbolic solution and wait. This special tank allows me to relax and enter a hypnotic state, enhancing my abilities. For now, I wait for our next clients. I see four chairs hooked up to my chamber. That means four guests, four fellow travelers. When I travel through time, they tell me only to look, not to touch anything, because to touch is to change destinies.

Jason Bray walks into the room. He sits at the monitor connected to my chamber. He smiles at me.

"How are you doing, Eliza?"

My first reaction is to say, "I'm floating in a sensory deprivation chamber like a big, high-tech angelfish. I'm about to take four total strangers on an intimate journey back in time to witness something horrible, something I must witness but can't change." But I know Jason is a good man and means well. He's always been very kind to me. I let the remark slide. I give him a smile.

"I am as good as can be expected, Jason. Thank you for asking."

Dr. Conners and Mr. Cash come into the travel area. Mr. Cash is a cold, hard man with a stern face and a fake head of hair. He acts as if he owns the place. He does. But he does not own me. He should not forget that. I have never met a man with a more fitting name.

Dr. Conners is a decent man with weary eyes. I think he believes that he is doing what he does for the good of science and for the world. Though he has changed over the years, I still believe his heart is in the right place. He taps on the glass of my chamber. "This is going to be an interesting group: a couple of psychologists from Berkeley and a couple of officials from the FAA. You'll be taking them to flight three one three one, a small commuter plane that went down last week between Buffalo and Cleveland."

"I read the briefing," I tell the doctor. "The professors are doing a study on fear and how humans react. The FAA people are hoping to learn what went wrong to prevent it from happening again."

"She is well prepared, as always. This will be quite a journey," says Cash with a smirk.

Dr. Conners smiles.

"Quite a journey, Mr. Cash?" I say bluntly as I float on the top of the tank. "I am going to witness people die and do nothing about it but watch. Not only that, I am going to be traveling through time and space with four other souls who will also witness this terrible event."

Mr. Cash takes a step back from my tank. "Yes, of course. It is a terrible loss of life. But with the data your fellow travelers collect, we can prevent future disasters. Let's care about the future and what we can do for humanity. You should be proud."

I nod. There is nothing I can do at this point. I wish we had better ways to help.

Mr. Cash clears his throat. He is the type of man who is not accustomed to people arguing with him.

02

Dr. Conners has an anxious grin on his face. He turns to one of the armed guards by the door. There are always armed guards around. It is a fact of life here. I don't like it, but I am used to it.

"Bring in Eliza's fellow travelers," Dr. Conners tells one of the guards.

I watch as the guard turns and leaves. I look at the door with anticipation. I am anxious to see those who will be traveling with me. The guard leads my fellow voyeurs, our clients, into the room. There are two men, one older with a white beard, the other younger and slim. There are two women, one tall with her hair in a bun and a stern look on her face, one short with short hair; she looks nervous. They are all dressed in special travel suits.

I am not sure which ones are the professors from Berkeley. I am not sure which ones are the FAA officials. It doesn't matter to me. It doesn't change my job, my mission. I am supposed to guide them, not psychoanalyze them.

The four travelers look in wonder at me floating in my hyperbolic tank. One of them, the short woman, even lets her jaw drop open. As they approach the tank, Dr. Conners gives his welcome speech.

"Greetings, I am Dr. Jeffery Conners," he says with a smile. He points to Mr. Cash. "I'm sure you all know Mr. Robert Cash, our founder and benefactor."

The four travelers bob their heads in polite agreement. They each give smiles of acknowledgment.

Dr. Conners turns toward me. The four look at me as if I am an exhibition in an aquarium.

"And this is Eliza. Eliza has the wonderful gift of astral projection. She is able to transport herself through time and space."

The four travelers look at me with a mix of curiosity and fear. I can sense their excitement and anticipation. Their thoughts pass through my mind.

Is it true? Can she really do that?

How did she develop these abilities?

They are about to see that I can, though I can only go as far back in time to the day I was born. It's one of my limitations. I'm not sure whether it is one I put on myself or one that time puts on me...I have yet to figure that out.

"Can she speak?" one of the women—the short one—asks, her hands shaking slightly.

I smile. "I can hear, talk, feel, and time travel. Trust me; this will be an experience like no other."

Mr. Cash gives me a look. He doesn't like me to speak too much. Besides, now it's time for his part of the speech. I am sure he and Dr. Conners practice this when nobody is around. "We have trained Eliza to time travel and share her abilities with others. She will take your minds on the voyage with her."

The four travelers look up at me. They look down at the chairs. I sense stray thoughts. They are skeptical and can't believe this is for real.

Is this a trick? Is this an illusion? Are we being hypnotized?

"I assure you—all this is real," I say. "I can see the universal strings that hold all matter together. I can move myself and my guests through those strings to certain places in time. I am your guide. You will be able to see, hear, and even smell the events. You just can't touch, because while you are there, you are not really physically there. Just your minds have traveled there through my mind."

"Fascinating," one of the men—the one with the beard—remarks.

Jason stands up from his monitor. He points to the four swivel chairs. "Please sit, and I will hook you up." He shows them a head brace with electrodes running through it. "While this may not look stylish, it is the latest in high-tech headgear."

The two men and the tall woman sit in their seats. The fourth traveler, the short woman, looks at the empty chair. She looks up at me. "What about you? Can you change things?"

"I too only observe," I tell her. Truthfully, I'm not sure if I can change events when I astral travel. Only time will tell.

The woman backs away from her chair, nervous, shaky. "I don't think I can do this," she shivers.

03

I look at the scared woman. She is shaking.

"What is your name?" I ask her. This is unusual for me. I do not wish to learn the names of my travelers. But I want to comfort this lady.

"My name is Lauren," she says meekly.

"Lauren, if you come with me, I guarantee this will be an experience you will never forget. It may not be easy on you, but you will get the answers you are searching for.

Lauren looks me in the eyes. I do not waver. She relaxes and takes her seat. Jason finishes hooking her up.

"Are there limits to where Eliza can travel to?" one of the men asks. I believe he is the professor.

Mr. Cash answers. "The further back in time she goes, the more strain that puts on her. So we restrict her to near-past events."

Dr. Conners looks over at the travelers. Jason makes sure each of them is properly wired up.

"Don't worry; it is absolutely safe, we have done this numerous times. Eliza has never lost a guest traveler."

"Can I be injured?" Lauren asks.

"Remember, your bodies will remain here; your astral form will travel with Eliza. You will be one hundred percent safe. Just remember the protocol: stay within sight of Eliza while you travel," Dr. Conners answers.

"What happens if we don't?"

"We may lose you!" snaps Cash with a smirk. "Forever…"

"He is joking," I tell them. "It is better if we stay close, because I have better control over my travelers. Our time is limited there, so I need to be sure I don't miss anyone on the way back."

The travelers all nod. I sense both their eagerness and their reluctance at the same time.

Dr. Conners picks up a newspaper and shows it to me. This helps me lock onto an event and stay focused on my destination. The headline reads, "31 Die in Plane Crash."

Dr. Conners gives me the details. "A month ago, on February 13, 2015, a small commuter plane took off from Buffalo, New York, at 6:32 p.m. eastern time. The plane crashed at 7:01 p.m. eastern time."

Jason activates a soft ringing sound, which only I can hear within my tank. This means it's time for me to go. The ringing sounds increase frequency, helping me to dissociate from my physical form into the mental domain.

I close my eyes. I let my mind drift deeper and deeper. Time becomes an object for me. The seconds, minutes, hours, days—all become strings of different lengths, different vibrations. I see them so clearly in my mind. I peel the strings away, creating an opening. I feel as if I am being pulled out of my body; the force is so strong and yet supporting. I hear the buzzing sounds become more pleasant, like thousands of tiny little bells ringing all at the same time. I slowly enter the opening of the tunnel, bringing my guests with me. I connect to them with the invisible strings I force myself to visualize and wrap around them. I take a deep breath. In a few seconds, we stream fast, and I visualize the date and time of the accident. Minutes before the crash, I command this time frame in my mind.

We are now standing in the middle of a passenger aircraft. It is a small plane with double seats on one side, singles on the other. I can sense it is 6:58 p.m. on February 13. All seems well; the thirty-one souls are so content.

"Fascinating," one of my FAA guests observes. "The wings of the plane are far too icy." He shakes his head. "They must have not deiced properly."

In the back row, I notice a young mother holding a small baby boy in her lap. He is not more than a year old. Yes, in fact I am correct; he is merely nine months old. The others all chose to be on this flight. The baby had no choice. I find that sad.

The plane starts to rumble, to sputter and shake. I look at the people. Some are scared. Some grab on to the armrests. Some are thinking, hoping, that this is just a little turbulence. A man and woman take each other's hands.

Now the plane starts shaking more violently. The nose of the plane jerks upward, suddenly, forcefully. Now, more of the passengers look scared. They are shaking, sweating, eyes locked open. Even the calmest now realize they are in danger.

The plane shakes harder, the rattling and vibrations pulsate through the passengers' bodies, causing even more fear.

The plane begins to plummet. I hear people scream.

This is like the time I rode the roller coaster at the park, but much worse. The plane spirals downward, spinning and spinning. The fear is thick. They all know they are going to die, all except the baby. The mother cradles her tight to her body. It will not help.

I should be watching my guests, but my eyes are fixed on the baby. I have observed death many times. It is my obligation, my duty, to watch but not to interfere. People die, but still live on in the thoughts of others. The universe continues. It is not my place to step in.

The ground is closer now. Impact is mere moments away. Everybody knows that, except the baby. Some people pray, others curse. One of them, an older man, has already expired from the shock.

I turn to look over at my travelers. They are fascinated and terrified.

"We are not really here," one of them mumbles to himself.

"You are here," I assure him, "just not in physical form."

The front of the plane shatters and bursts into flames. The fire sweeps through the hull, transforming all it engulfs to charred husks. Their pain is intense but short.

I look at the baby in the back. The flames are about to engulf him and his mother.

04

I continue to stare at the lady and her precious baby boy. I know they have only moments left alive. The FAA people come forward; I think they got what they needed. The rest of the group is trying to capture whatever they need for their study on the human emotion of fear.

I think about the baby. I take a deep breath and then another. The flames are eating through the cabin, devouring all they touch. I think more about the baby. I take another breath. I hold out my hand.

I move closer to the baby, without losing sight of my passengers. The poor, sweet, innocent little soul. My mind reaches out to the near infinity that is the universe. I parse through the strings that connect this baby, this little soul, with the rest of all that there is. I'm tempted to look forward, to the future, to see what this baby may become. I don't. I do not want to know. I do know this baby is innocent. This baby did not choose to be here. I wonder if I can make it so this baby was never here.

I close my eyes. I visualize alternate possible realities. I picture the baby and his mom leaving their home and heading to the airport. Scanning their timelines quickly, I see the baby has a father who stayed at home to work while the infant and his mother went to visit her mother. I wish the baby had stayed home with the father. I try to see this reality bend the current reality to it. I command this reality to take priority. I visualize many different possible trajectories for this baby, like branches on a tree, all representing plausible pathways for his life. I replace the current with a lower branch, one where the baby stays home with his father.

The flames engulf all, all but myself and my passengers.

"Please stop this! I wanna go back!" one of my passengers pleads.

I look at her, and she is white with terror. All of my passengers are scared now. It is unpleasant to see people about to die. My heart is breaking.

I take a deep breath. It is time to go back. I force the strings to wrap around each of my passengers. It's not easy, due to their moving and shaking. I have to make sure I don't leave anyone behind. I increase the strength of the strings that bind us, and pull into the tunnel streaming back to the lab.

I am back in my tank, floating, my passengers safe in their chairs. I sigh in relief.

Dr. Conners and some medics attend to them. Each of the passengers is just sitting there, eyes wide open.

"Stay seated," Dr. Conners tells them. "Astral traveling through time can be draining. We will have medics check you out and administer fluids if needed."

I float up to the ladder connected to the top of my tank. Jason climbs up the ladder to help me out. He extends his hand for me. Every time he does that, I feel reassured and welcome. I wonder if he knows that.

"How was it?" Jason asks.

"Sad," I tell him as I climb onto the ladder.

Jason starts down, and I follow.

"Of course it's sad; thirty lives were lost in that crash," Jason says.

"Yes," I nod. I think back to the headline. It had read thirty-one. Did this work? Did I really save the baby?

I turn my attention to my four fellow travelers. They are still weak, tired, and confused.

As I pass by Lauren, she reaches up and takes my hand. "How are you, Eliza?" she asks. I look at her. She continues, "Something extraordinary happened on the plane, didn't it?"

"Yes, you got to experience the past," I tell her.

Mr. Cash and Dr. Conners both smile at me. They like my answer.

Lauren trembles. "No, no something else happened. Something different. I felt it. I was terrorized, but then suddenly I felt like there was a bit of light among all the death."

"All death is a new beginning—it's cycle of life. Maybe that's what you mean by light among death," says Dr. Conners.

"You need rest, Lauren. This is a metaphysical reality, and it can have an effect on your mind and your body," I tell her.

She nods.

Jason wraps a towel around my shoulders.

"How are you feeling?" Dr. Conners asks.

"I'm a little tired," I answer.

He nods. "That's understandable." He points toward the exit. "Jason will escort you to your quarters to relax."

I turn and walk toward the exit. I stumble just a little. Jason lunges for me and keeps me from falling. I lean on him, letting him guide me toward the exit.

Jason and I enter the long hallway. I have been down this dim corridor hundreds of times, but this is the first time I've ever noticed that the walls are light blue. I don't know why.

We walk in silence for a few minutes. Finally, Jason blurts, "You've made twenty-two trips since I've been here. Yet I've never seen you or your travelers so shaken up."

"Well, watching thirty people die like that was horrible," I say.

"Thirty-one, Eliza. You are tired…"

"Oh, right, thirty-one," I say.

We reach the door to my room.

05

Jason and I stand outside the door to my quarters. The number *thirty* echoes in my mind. Is my mind playing tricks on me? Taunting me? When I got on the plane, my mind told me there were thirty-one people on board. Yet now only thirty perished in flames. I should be happy if, indeed, what I wanted to happen actually happened: I saved the baby. I changed one's fate for good.

Jason points to my door. "Well, you get some rest. I'm sure Dr. Conners and Mr. Cash will be debriefing you first thing in the morning."

"Oh, joy," I tell him, forcing my weak smile to curl upward.

"Remember, if you need anything, I'm just a buzz away," Jason tells me.

That comforts me some. I wish I could tell him more, but looking at the cameras monitoring the hallway, I am stifled to express how I feel. I give him a warm smile.

Jason sees me glancing at the cameras. "You know, those cameras are for your safety," he assures me. "Remember, the outside world is dangerous, Eliza. We want to keep you protected." For some reason every time he speaks of the outside world being dangerous, his face cringes a little. I sense his discomfort. Is it because he feels the unpleasantness of that world? Or is he lying? I want to believe he is on my side.

I lean on my door. "So, I've been told." I open the door. Turning to Jason, I tell him, "Traveling always drains me some. I need to get my rest."

Jason smiles and leaves.

I walk into my quarters and shut the door. My quarters really aren't much—a bed, a desk with a computer, bookshelves, a closet. Pretty basic. From what I understand, it's much like your typical college dorm room.

I go into the bathroom and remove my wetsuit. I enter the shower and let the water rush over me. I am hoping the pulsating spray will relax my body and my mind.

I leave the shower, wrap a towel around myself, and lie down on my bed. I need to relax and sleep. I try, but I can't. Between excitement and worry, I feel I need to distract myself.

I sit up and go to my computer. I know they limit my access to the Internet, but they will still allow me to look at the crash information. After all, the more I know about a situation I am traveling to, the easier it is for me to travel there. Reports from all over the country appear on my screen. I scan the names, and there are thirty of them. No mention of a baby dying. I changed time. What will this do to me? The rest of us? The future?

I'm so anxious that I need to be around people. Looking at the clock, I see that it is 12:50 a.m. The other guests will still be at the cafeteria, even though it's late. These people are all night owls. Their minds are too busy to sleep, always working, processing, bending, never shutting down. I want to join them.

By the time I dress and get to the cafeteria, it is close to 1:00 a.m. The cafeteria is the one public place in this complex that is brightly lit and colored.

When I enter, I feel all eyes turn to me. On days I travel, it is big news here. There are other special people around, but none of them can time travel and enter parallel worlds. I walk through the food line, choosing a salad and some water. I find it is best to eat a little after I travel, even if it's late. It gives me energy. They serve food here 24-7. I scan the room for a place to sit. There, sitting at one long table, are Bob, Tom, Lily, and Cindy.

Walking over to their table, I ask, "May I sit with you?"

"Of course," Cindy answers. She is a young, slim girl with long blond hair and deep-blue eyes. She is clairvoyant; she can channel information almost like a human Google.

"How can we say no to the queen of the building?" Lily sneers as I sit across from her.

"I am not a queen," I state.

Lily locks her glare on me. She is older than I am, but not by much. She has dark hair, a dark complexion, and perhaps even a darker mind. She is empathic, and she can feel what others feel. She can also project her feelings and thoughts onto others. She has been used for some special operations. Everyone is secretive here, and they are all quite good at guarding strategic information from one another.

Tom is a younger man, short and slim. He points at a saltshaker. It moves across the table to me. He is telekinetic. "Salt?" he asks with a smile, trying to break the tension between Lily and me.

"No thanks," I say.

Bob sits back in his chair. He is older, and what hair he has left is gray. He has a long nose and long fingers that he is always fiddling with. Mindreading is probably his strongest talent.

"We understand you had quite the trip today," Bob tells me.

Yes, as always," I respond.

Suddenly I feel someone probing my mind. I block whoever is trying to scan me.

Tom looks at me with wide eyes. "Yes, but this trip was extra interesting. We heard one of your travelers freaked out!"

"One woman panicked," I say calmly. "It's understandable. What we saw was sad."

"Must have been terrible," Cindy says, trembling a bit as if she is channeling this woman's energy.

I try to stay calm, yet still feel another mind trying to reach into my mind, attempting to read my thoughts and feelings.

"From what I understand, this woman who panicked was upset by more than the death and destruction," Bob says, probing me with his words, trying to gain some sort of reaction.

I shrug. "She simply panicked and misread the situation. That's all there is to it," I tell him.

"If that's all, then why are you here now?" Lily asks. "Usually after you travel you rest for hours, and we don't see you until the next day. Does something bother you?"

I feel the other mind pushing harder and harder. I can't determine who is doing the pushing…but I know what they are looking for. I do not appreciate the attack on my privacy.

06

I feel the attacker pressing my mind, probing it. It is as if millions of tiny surgical knives are trying to cut their way into my subconscious. I imagine my mind as a steel safe with thick walls: impenetrable. Nothing gets in or out unless I will it to. Still, the attack continues, pressing, pushing, looking for a chink in my mental armor.

I lean back in my chair calmly. Putting my arms behind my head to show how relaxed I am, I smile. I look at Bob, Tom, Cindy, and Lily, trying to decipher which one of them is probing me.

"Today's trip was eventful and a little draining," I admit. "That is why I am here now. I needed both food and the comfort of my friends," I say, hoping they leave me alone.

Cindy leans forward and puts her hand over my hand. "Take it easy, sister; we are here for you," she says earnestly.

Could this be a feint, a fake by Cindy? Could she be the one probing me? I don't believe so. Still, I can't be certain. Not yet at least.

My attacker changes strategy. Instead of blasting my mind from every conceivable angle, he or she tries a concentrated attack. He or she combines all the little mental knives that were trying to cut and dice me into one giant attack. The initial attack was just a probe, looking for weak spots. The attacker thinks he or she has found one and is now concentrating all his or her energy on that spot to drill and bore into my mind.

My attacker is being foolish if he or she thinks I really have an opening.

"Yes, Eliza, we are all here for you," Tom says. He turns to Bob and Lily. "Right, guys?"

Bob nods. "Sure, I guess," he mumbles. "I just want what's best for everyone," he says slowly. "Besides, I know what it's like be shunned for being different." He stops for a moment, pulls out a knife, and cuts a slice of cheese. He eats the cheese off the knife and then notes, "All I want to do is help the world to be a better place."

"That's why we are here—to learn how to use our abilities wisely," Cindy says.

"Yes," Tom adds. "Plus the facility is forming some focus groups to help learn the best way to tell the world about us."

Lily sneers. "Oh, please, Tom, tell us more about how they are trying to unveil us to the world in a soft, user-friendly manner. I've heard that story for years. They still haven't come up with a way to do it." She shakes her head and snickers.

The attack on my mind continues. They have shifted tactics again after the direct approach failed. Whoever it is, they are using smaller, wisp-like attacks. Their strikes are fast and crisp, as they seek to slip in through a crack in my defenses. Each attack is repelled.

I notice a few beads of sweat forming on Lily's forehead.

"So, what's going on between you and Jason?" Cindy asks sincerely. "I notice he spends a lot more time with you than anybody else."

"Jason is a friend," I tell her.

Lily rolls her eyes.

The pressure of the mental probe becomes stronger. It hurts. Time to strike back. I take all that mental energy that has been pounding at me, and I gather it in my mind. I shape it into a giant glowing ball, adding my mental energy, making it pulsate and vibrate, heightening the frequency. I then deflect the ball back toward the source of the attack.

Lily darts back in her chair. It figures that she was the one. She puts her hands up to her eyes and grimaces in pain. Her face is red, her hair disheveled.

"What's wrong, Lily?" Tom asks.

"Nothing," Lily says, still holding her hands to her head. "Nothing, just a migraine."

I stand up from the table. "While I appreciate the company, my friends," I say as I stare at Lily, "it's been a long day."

07

I head to my room. It really has been a long, tiring, strange day. Either my abilities are growing, or I am going insane. Perhaps it is a little of both.

Reaching my room, I let myself collapse on my bed. I close my eyes and try to remove all thoughts from my mind. I want to clear my head and just sleep. My mind is racing though. I take a deep breath and then another. I relax my body.

Images of my mother and father ripple through my mind. I see my father and his smile. My mother and her warm eyes. It's been years since their deaths in the car crash and my waking up in the hospital to learn they were gone. They were both taken from me so quickly, without warning. Now they are just memories.

Sometimes I wish I could go back to the time before the crash and stop it. But something has always blocked me.

My powers, for better or for worse, started to manifest themselves right after I lost my parents. I was left alone, no other family. I went from one foster home to another. I used to daydream to help me deal with my sadness and loneliness. I felt no one was there for me anyway. I daydreamed so intensely that I found myself dissociating into parallel realities that seemed like fiction to me. They felt so safe and pleasant. I saw different beings, angel-like creatures and elves in beautiful, lush, green forests with the brightest blue sky and the most warming sun.

Whether it was real or not, all I cared was that these inexplicable places were so healing.

Jason always says that time is tricky and filled with loopholes and contradictions. I wonder—if I went back and changed the accident, then perhaps I would never have had these powers. Of course, then I would never have been able to use these powers to change the event that gave me these powers. It's a paradox for sure. Possibly, that is why I mentally avoid traveling to that place in my life.

Then again, would losing my powers be a bad thing? I would be normal and just like everybody else, out in the world and free. Maybe this outside world wouldn't be so dangerous anymore. I need to stop thinking and sleep. I start visualizing numbers going backward: 200, deeper, 199, I relax more, 198, deeper and deeper. Soothing relaxation slowly spreads throughout my body, every limb, muscle, and fiber. I drift into the void, feeling so comfortable now, 197, 196, numbers going into nothing, nothing, nothing…

Suddenly, I hear a rustling noise outside my door. There is somebody there in the hallway. The guards are down on the far ends. They never come to my door. .

"Hello? Who's out there?" I call out.

No reply. Yet I still feel the presence of someone. Reaching for the knob, I open the door.

Bob is standing there, a blank look on his face.

"Bob, what are you doing here?" I demand.

Suddenly, he grabs me by the throat. He pushes forward, forcing me back into the room.

"Bob! What are you doing?" I scream.

He drives me to the ground.

"What you did was wrong!" he shouts from on top of me. "I must stop you for the world."

He has a knife in his right hand, and it is coming closer and closer to my chest. He is trying to plunge it into my heart. I'm trying to stop him, but I can't. He is much bigger than I am and has the advantage. Still, I need to fight back. If I don't stop him, I am dead.

08

"Stop, Bob!" I scream at him.

His eyes are unblinking, locked on me. "I know what you did, Eliza. You want to change the world around you, don't you?" he says calmly, though still trying to plunge the knife into my chest.

"Bob, I have no idea what you are talking about."

"You know what I am talking about! What you did on the plane was selfish."

"Bob, whatever happened on the plane happened out of goodwill."

Bob rolls his eyes, "Look at you, so arrogant."

"Help!" I call out to the guards.

Bob smiles calmly. "They will not be here in time. The cameras are off."

I try to push his arm upward, but he is being driven by rage and fear, and he has the advantage of being on top.

"Bob, if you finish my life, your life will be over too," I tell him.

"Oh yeah?" says Bob. "All they care about is our abilities and not our crimes. I will live just as fine and be better off if you were gone. We'll all be better off."

Bob increases the pressure he is applying to the knife. My arms are growing tired. I am fighting a losing battle.

I feel the tip of the knife make contact with my body. I have very little time left.

I reach into Bob's mind. I need to jolt him like I did Lily. It is so hard to concentrate, though, with Bob applying all this pressure. I picture reaching into Bob's mind with my hand and twisting the nerves of his brain. I have no choice.

Bob pulls back, releasing his grip on me. He puts a hand to his forehead. "Ah, that hurt me, you bitch!" he shouts.

"You think that hurt," I tell him. I force my knee up, hitting him hard between his legs. I'm glad I had been working on self-defense techniques with Jason.

Bob rolls off me, groaning in pain, holding his hands between his legs. He releases the knife and lets it drop to the floor.

I hear the guards coming down the hallway.

Bob grabs the knife and lashes at me. I got too close, the knife cuts into my gown, and through to my skin. Placing my hand over the wound, I feel blood. I walk backward quickly. Looking down at the wound, I see that, fortunately, it is only superficial. Still, Bob is lunging at me again, waving the knife wildly.

I don't have a lot of time. I need to picture Bob's heart in my mind. His mind is too well guarded now. His heart—not a single fence or wire around it. I see his heart, pulsating, beating, filling with blood, and then sending that blood out to the rest of his body. It is pulsating quickly. He is anxious, excited…I picture that heart skipping a bit…stopping…stopping. Stop!

Bob drops the knife and places his hand over his chest. He crumbles to the ground.

The guards burst into the room. "Eliza, we're sorry; somehow the security cameras were offline," one of them says.

They look at Bob lying there on the floor. "What happened?" the other guard asks.

"Bob attacked me," I say as calmly as I can. "I struggled. I believe I got lucky as he may have had a heart attack."

09

I look down at Bob lying there helpless on the floor. He could be dead from what I did. I just wanted him to leave me alone.

A couple of medics rush into the room, carrying medical bags. One of them, a young woman with bright-green eyes, comes to my side. The other, an older man, drops down to Bob's side.

"Eliza, are you OK?" the medic with the bright eyes asks me.

"Bob attacked her," one of the guards tells the medic.

"I am fine," I insist.

The medic working on Bob takes his pulse and listens to his lungs.

I tell the medic with the bright eyes, "Please help Bob…"

One of the guards pats me on the shoulder. "You are a good woman, Eliza. This man attacked you, and yet you care about him."

Looking down at Bob, I feel bad about what happened, but I'm glad I'm alive.

Dr. Conners comes rushing into the room. Jason follows closely on his heels. Three more security people flank them, with guns drawn.

"Tell me what happened here!" Dr. Conners orders the guards.

The medics have torn Bob's shirt open and have connected him to a defibrillator.

"Bob had some kind of breakdown and attacked Eliza," one of the first security people tells Dr. Conners.

"How did this happen?" Dr. Conners asks angrily. "Why didn't the security camera pick this up right away?"

One of the security people takes a step backward. His gaze falls away from Dr. Conners. "We don't know, sir. Somehow the cameras were all taken offline. We corrected the problem immediately."

Dr. Conners shakes his head. "Mr. Cash will not be happy. This malfunction is unacceptable."

"He has no heartbeat and isn't breathing. We need to shock him," one of the medics informs Dr. Conners.

"Do it!" he tells them.

"Clear!" the medics shout.

The sound of the defibrillator charging fills the room. As they jolt him, Bob's body trembles like a fish forced out of water.

I shake my head. Poor Bob. If he had just left me alone, none of this would have happened.

Jason puts a blanket around me. It's a nice gesture even though I am not cold.

"Are you OK, Eliza?" he asks.

Dr. Conner takes out a penlight and flashes it in my eyes. "Please, follow the light, Eliza," he asks.

I concentrate on the light. It helps me take my mind off Bob.

"Still no sinus rhythm!" I hear one of the medics say.

"Shock him again," Dr. Conners orders them while still paying attention to me.

The sound of the defibrillator once again fills the room.

"Clear!"

I hear a zap, the thud of Bob's body bouncing off the floor, again. Then a steady, beep, beep, beep...

"We have a heartbeat," one of the medics says. "It's weak and thready, but it's there."

Dr. Conners is still more interested in my eyes than Bob. "Fine. Have him moved to the infirmary ASAP." Dr. Conners pulls the light away.

He turns to Jason. "Eliza seems fine. She should be ready for our debriefing as planned."

Jason takes a step forward toward Dr. Conners, positioning himself between me and the doctor.

"Dr. Conners, I think Eliza could use extra rest before she goes through her debrief," Jason says, "especially after what just happened."

"Jason, do you have a medical degree, or is there something else on your mind?" Dr. Conners asks.

Jason looks back at Conners. "It's just humane. Besides, she's our primary asset. We need her to be in her best condition."

Two more medics arrive at my doorway with a stretcher. They are about to remove Bob.

Dr. Conners looks past Jason to me. "Eliza, we shall see you in three hours."

With those words, Dr. Conners turns and leaves the room.

I look at Jason. "I don't think one extra hour will make that much of a difference, but I appreciate you standing up for me."

Everybody leaves. I feel distraught yet relieved that the chaos has calmed down. I lie down on my bed, and I think of Jason. I know he cares about me. Perhaps there is something more here. He's the only one in this entire facility that I feel totally comfortable with. I want to talk to him without cameras in the room. When I look him in the eyes, I think he wants the same. I let my mind wander. I'm curious what it would feel like to be in the room with him, just the two of us. Would he comfort me? Would he want to stay with me? I drift off thinking of Jason. Pleasant thoughts lull me to sleep

10

After a couple of hours, Jason greets me at my door with a cup of fresh coffee.

A few minutes later we are in a private lounge near the debriefing room. I am anxious and worried but trying not to show it.

"Were you able to get some sleep?" Jason asks.

I take a sip of the coffee. "Yes," I tell him, blushing just a little, knowing how soothing thoughts of him helped me fall asleep.

Jason looks at me and says, "You know, I'm impressed with the way you handled everything. From that Lauren woman in your last trip and then Bob…"

"Thank you," I tell him.

"How are you and Lily getting along?" Jason asks me.

After all that has happened these last few hours, I find that to be an interesting question. I grin. "Lily and I have always had a complicated relationship."

Two security guards walk into the lounge. "Excuse me, Eliza, Jason— Dr. Conners and Mr. Cash would like to see you now in Room M1," one of the guards tells us.

"Please come with us," the other guard says.

"Room M1?" Jason looks puzzled. "Why there?"

The guards both shake their heads. "We don't ask questions; we just do what we are told."

I stand up. "It's OK, Jason, I want to get this over with."

I walk toward the guards.

The guards escort Jason and me out of the lounge, down another long dim hallway. "Why have I never been in room M1 before?" I ask.

"It's a classified room," Jason tells me, more rigid than usual.

I lean into Jason and whisper, "Jason, please, tell me what's in there?"

"It's an fMRI, the latest in lie detection science," he says. "I'm not sure why we are going there. I just received an order a few minutes ago."

Jason and I walk in silence. Finally, after what seems to be hours but is really just minutes, we come to a large, windowless metal door. One of the guards presses some buttons on the keypad at the side of the door, and it pops open.

"Go in, please," the guard says.

Jason and I walk into the room. It's a large, lab-type space broken up into two areas. The front area has a long table and chairs with bright overhead lights. Sitting at that table are Dr. Conners, Mr. Cash, and Lily. Why in the hell would Lily be here? I notice the back of the room has a control panel and an observation area that overlooks a large tubular machine.

"Thank you for coming, Eliza," Mr. Cash says. He points to the chair across the table from the three of them. "Please sit."

Conners looks at Jason. "Jason, you will be in charge of the fMRI today."

Jason looks at Dr. Conners and Mr. Cash with surprise. Jason and I exchange a glance, then he heads to the other part of the room.

"What's this all about?" I ask as I sit down.

Dr. Conners smiles at me. "Eliza, we have another mission for you, another chance for you to travel. Have you heard of the Brighter Day Cult in Wyoming?"

"I'm familiar with them," I say.

"Well, they have been stockpiling arms for years. Early today they shot and killed a sheriff who was on a routine call there. They have de-clared their land as a sovereign state. They have also taken a few locals hostage. The FBI needs to shut them down now!" Dr. Conners informs me.

"Eliza, your abilities make you the ultimate information-collecting machine. You are more accurate than any satellite, drone, or infrared camera. You can visit the camp and report on the personnel they have, where the hostages are, and how well armed the followers are. You can make the FBI's job much easier," Mr. Cash says.

"Still, why I am in this room, and why is Lily here?" I ask.

"That's where this gets touchy," Mr. Cash admits. "After what happened to Bob, Lily came to us. She told us she has been picking up some very weird readings from you after your last trip. She also told us that Bob said to her that you changed something in the past…"

I sit back in my seat. My heart is pounding. I take a deep breath, then another. "I can't change the events when I travel."

"That's what we've always believed," Dr. Conners says. "Changing past events should be impossible…"

"I agree with Bob; your vibe has been off since the last time trip," Lily says coolly.

I look down at the table. "It wasn't easy watching all those people die…"

Dr. Conners reaches across the table and puts a hand on my shoulder. "Of course it wasn't. But now you have a chance to save many lives. Only, before you do that, we need to make sure we can trust you."

"Of course you can trust me. I only want to help," I insist.

"Good, then you should have no problem taking this MRI," says Dr. Conners with a smile.

This place is getting on my nerves. If they detect that I have something to hide, they will punish and try to brainwash me, like they did to Cindy last year for complaining too much. They used magnetic waves to alter her perception against her will and make her more cooperative. Now she's like a sheep. I don't want to become like her…

11

"OK, Eliza, the MRI is ready; you may follow the guard," Dr. Conners tells me as one of the guards walks over to escort me to the machine.

I do not move.

Lily points at me. "See, she hesitates. She's scared. She's hiding something."

I want to lash out and make Lily be quiet, but I don't want to make things worse.

Once again, I feel Lily is probing inside my head. She is trying to use the situation to take advantage of my defenses being down. I concentrate on not letting her in. I visualize a shield around me, but her probing feels like arrows, energetic spears trying to invade me. Why is she doing this? Does she want me to hurt, to lose my mind? I don't understand this. Isn't it enough I am already here about to go into this lie detector machine? She got what she wanted. But she won't stop. I feel a jolt. She is good. Too bad I am so weak. I have no power to fight back. I feel myself boiling now. My anger is getting stronger. I need to calm down and just deal with everything as is.

I close my eyes and breathe deeply, so deeply that I feel my anxiety beginning to leave me. I wish I could escape away from this chaos to someplace safe. Just for a moment…it seems like my anger is dissipating, too. But my wishes take over…someplace away…away from here I think.

Surprisingly, as the anger is leaving me, it's also pushing me forward, forward, out of my body, almost like a powerful force. Little did I know that anger could serve as power. Like a rocket almost, I am streaming out...someplace else. I want peace.

I see a bright tunnel opening up in front of me; streaks of energy line each side of the tunnel. I begin to feel some relief. The light from the tunnel is warm and inviting. I feel myself being pulled in, floating, flying, streaming toward the end of this beautiful glorious tunnel. In the back of my mind, I hear Lily's voice, "No! Stop! You can't do this!" I ignore her.

The next thing I know I am standing in a beautiful, wide-open field. The sun shines warmly in a rich blue sky. I am surrounded by butterflies, circling unusually large red, violet, and yellow flowers. The aroma is so sweet and soothing. As I walk, I feel soft grass beneath my feet. I kick off my shoes and let the grass squish between my toes. It is quiet and peaceful here. Looking around, I smile when I see white doves circling in the air and furry gray little bunnies hopping to and fro.

I just want to stay here forever. But I can't, I must go back, back to the gruesomely harsh reality and face my choices. Yes, if they detect I lied, they will punish me. After all, maybe Bob and Lily are right...Maybe I am dangerous...I have made bad choices. Or am I losing my mind? I feel fear rushing over me, unpleasantly tingling negative energy entering my every cell and fiber; it makes me nauseous.

The sky darkens, as if some mad painter is harshly covering it with thick gray strokes. As I look down, I see the flowers turn into withering, dying plants, wilting beneath my feet, and the grass melting into mud. The animals are all gone; all I see are worms and spiders crawling toward me. I hear a strange, high-pitched shriek in the air. Looking up, I see giant dark black bats bearing down on me. I cry for help.

"Eliza, you are going to be all right," I hear a very familiar voice, so soothing and comforting.

I turn around, and I see the image of my mother standing next to me. She is emanating light and peace.

"Mom, what are you doing here?"

She smiles at me. "You, my dear daughter, can do anything and be anywhere...You create your own realities." She concentrates and opens her arms wide and creates a shield of glowing light energy all around, separating us from the darkness. I feel safe again and curious at the same time.

Her smile widens. "See, anything is possible. It all starts with directing the flow of our feelings and emotions. If you can control them, you will create anything you want. Your power to affect realities is far beyond normal. Dr. Conners and Mr. Cash told your father and me that our children would be exceptional, but I never dreamed you would be this formidable."

"Wait? You know Dr. Conners and Mr. Cash?"

My mother nods. "Yes, my love, you were far from an accident."

12

"I don't understand. How could you know Dr. Conners?" I take a deep breath. "I didn't even meet him until I was fourteen and in a foster home."

My mother looks away from me. It is obvious that she does not want to tell me what really happened. But in this strange reality no words are needed. I can hear her talk to me telepathically. I feel her emotions and they become my knowledge.

My mother looks at me lovingly. I hear her speak without moving her mouth. "Your father and I were part of a study Dr. Conners did while we were freshmen in college. Dr. Conners said he was looking for genetic markers for people prone to psychosis. Whoever was enrolled in the study would have to report back to him once a year. The study paid a good deal of money. It helped pay for college for many kids."

"Wait, you knew Dad when you were freshmen?" I ask.

Mom drops her head again. "No, we didn't know each other during those studies." She shakes her head and then goes silent.

At this moment, I feel discomfort from her, making it hard for me to read her.

My mother continues slowly. "After the initial study, Dr. Conners approached your father and me. He told us he would pay us an obscene amount of money if we simply had a child together." She pauses for a minute to catch her breath and collect her thoughts. "He said that our genes had a specific formula and that if we had a child, it would be some sort of genius with special mental abilities. But he would have to follow the child for a lifelong psychological research study, for which he would pay us enormous money. He assured us the child would have the best of everything."

"Mother, no...."

For the first time, my mother smiles. She reaches out and touches me gently on the arm. "I must admit, we were tempted, so tempted. But your father and I didn't know each other at the time and were total strangers; plus selling our child to a study was so wrong. Dr. Conners said he understood and if we ever change our minds to let him know. The offer would always stand."

"So, you changed your mind?" I ask, unable to read her anymore. "You had me and you gave me to them?" I am ready to cry.

My mother shakes her head, her eyes filled with wonder. "No, my love." My mother's smile widens. "After meeting in the lab, your father and I realized we liked each other. We became friends. That friendship blossomed into a romance. That romance would create you..." My mother pauses, collecting her thoughts. "We never told Dr. Conners about you. We left town and settled far away from the university."

My mother looks me in the eyes. "We never suspected that a university professor would have the type of resources needed to follow us, track us..."

I look down, angry at the lab and what they did. They tracked them down. Well, at least I was born. And born out of my parent's will; no one forced them. But my parents are dead, and I am at the lab. I look and see my mother is gone and so is the shield. The bats are bearing down on me. I can feel the force from their beating wings. I know I have a choice: to get sucked into my anger, or let it dissolve. It's hard. I feel betrayed.

I follow my mom's advice—I choose a new reality. I know these bats are nothing more than fears, anger, and frustration. I choose to let go and forgive. Even though I have many more questions, unanswered, I release my frustration. I breathe in deep, exhaling my tension slowly. I let the thoughts of anger dissipate. Suddenly, the giant, horse-sized bats shrink, their wings and bodies morph before my eyes. I hold out my hand. Two little blue butterflies land on my index finger.

I shake my hand, and the butterflies float away. I feel the beams from the sun bathing me in their warmth. I smell fresh grass. The sounds of birds chirping fill the air.

It's time to return and face my reality at the lab. I am ready. As I think that, suddenly I am engulfed back in the tunnel, streaming back to my original reality. I will be face to face with Conners and Cash in only a few precious moments...

13

I feel myself streaming back toward my reality, my time. Opening my mind's eye, I can see all the points in time unfold before me. I see the room I was in—Dr. Conners, Lily, and I are sitting at the table. Jason is walking toward the MRI machine. No, this is not the moment I want to return to. I need to return to a time before that, just a few moments before I got overwhelmed with their questions and Lily's probing attacks. I mentally flip through the folds of time a bit more. I see myself and Jason walking into the special interrogation room. I choose that point in time to return to.

The next thing I know, I'm walking into the interrogation room with Jason. I feel totally calm and relaxed. I see Dr. Conners, Mr. Cash, and Lily sitting at the table, waiting for us.

"Thank you for coming, Eliza," Mr. Cash says. He points to the chair across the table from the three of them. "Please sit."

Dr. Conners looks at Jason. "Jason, you will be in charge of the fMRI today."

I gaze at the cold, sterile MRI at the back of the room. I no longer fear taking the MRI test. I realize I can easily beat it. No matter what they ask me, I feel good about myself. I did everything right. I saved the baby; I did good. I protected myself from crazy Bob; I did good. Maybe even others are safer now.

Looking at Lily, I see her back is rigid and her eyes are locked on me. She must sense something is different. I ignore her probe. She has about as much of a chance of penetrating my defenses as a mosquito does of hurting a rhino. Right now, Lily is no more than a simple annoyance.

Dr. Conners smiles at me. "Eliza, we have another mission for you. Another chance for you to travel. Have you heard of the Brighter Day Cult in Wyoming?"

"Yes," I say.

"Well, they have been stockpiling arms for years. Early today they shot and killed a sheriff who was on a routine call there. They have declared their land as a sovereign state. They have also taken a few locals hostage. The FBI needs to shut them down now," Dr. Conners tells me, not knowing I have lived through this moment before.

"The mission sounds like a worthwhile one," I state.

Dr. Conners, Mr. Cash, and Lily stand up. Mr. Cash turns toward the machine. "Then let's go join Jason at the MRI so we can clear you for this."

When we reach the back of the room, Jason takes me by the hand and escorts me onto the long patient table that will roll me into the machine. As he makes sure I am secure on the table, Jason leans into me and whispers, "I'm sure you will do fine, Eliza. Just keep cool."

I slide into the machine and take a deep breath. I think about what my mother said: "We create our realities." I am pure, and I have nothing to fear. My thoughts direct my reality.

The machine lights up and roars to life. I find the clanking annoying, but I block it from my mind. I concentrate on my answers. *Is your name Eliza? Did you do anything out of the ordinary on your last trip? Did you put Bob into a coma?* I feel as if I am trancing out as I answer their questions. Every question leads to an honest and innocent answer. I say, *My name is Eliza...I did nothing out of the ordinary.* In my mind I know that saving a baby is quite ordinary for me. *I didn't put Bob into coma,* I answer. As I think, it was his body that put him into coma. And so on and on, I answer in that same fashion. I remain cool and calm.

I feel like time goes by fast, so fast, minutes become seconds, seconds become milliseconds, as if I am fast-forwarding through the moments. Next thing I know I hear Jason say, "She passed…All clear."

I roll out of the machine. I did it.

Jason walks over to me and offers his hand. "See, that wasn't so bad."

I sit up.

Dr. Conners and Mr. Cash each glare at Lily, who leans backward. I hear Mr. Cash tell Lily, "We'll talk about this tomorrow."

Dr. Conners walks up to me, smiling. "Very good, Eliza; now go get some rest," he says. "We will call you when we are ready for you to travel to spy on the cult."

Jason looks at me, and his face is so kind.

"Eliza, may I escort you back to your room?" he asks, offering me his arm.

I take his arm and say, "I would love that."

14

Jason and I are walking down the hallway toward my room.
"I was impressed by you back there. I don't know how you handle the pressure in this place," Jason tells me with a warm smile.

"What do you know about the pressure?" I ask him. He looks at the cameras. I sense he wants to tell me something but cannot. I try to read his mind. What is it? I wonder...does he know something I don't? How many more secrets can there be? I look closely at him. Our eyes lock, and I hear him say, "I am on your side; we need a safe place to talk."

I am excited, relieved, and yet worried—all at the same time. Never in a million years would I have believed that Jason and I could communicate telepathically. I am worried about what he is trying to tell me, so I try to connect with him deeper. He is right; we need a safe place...

I lean into Jason, trying to establish connection. That feels rather warm and sweet.

Suddenly, Jason staggers backward and grabs his head.

I move forward, steadying him by the shoulder. "Jason, what's wrong..."

"I don't know," he grimaces meekly. "My head...such pain...."

I put my palm on his forehead. I can feel the pain coursing through him, surging through each of his nerves, jolting his muscles. This is not natural pain. He is being mentally assaulted. I use my mind to reach into his mind. I need to sense who is responsible for this attack. I am pretty certain I know, but I can't lash out until I am sure.

I close my eyes and let my conscious guide me to whoever is attacking Jason. Of course, I see Lily—well, a representation of Lily—she is holding a brain in her hand and squeezing it. Our minds lock. I'm not sure if I am in Lily's mind or we are both in Jason's mind. It does not matter.

"Lily, stop!" I say mentally.

She continues to squeeze it even harder.

"Why harm Jason? He has done nothing to you."

Lily continues. "You think you are better than anybody else here? That you can fool everyone? Well, watch how you lose your cool now, bitch. By the time I am done with him, his mind will be mush."

"You know I can't let you do that…"

Lily laughs. "You're not traversing through time now, Eliza. You are on the mental plane. This is where I am at my strongest!"

I curl my fingers into fists. "Foolish Lily, this may be where you are strongest, but even here you still pale to me."

"Let's see about that!" Lily shouts.

Lily waves her hand. A tornado forms and whips out at me. The force of the winds crashes into me. Lily is strong. But I cannot let her win, or Jason is doomed. I picture in my mind Lily's tornado dissipating into a small refreshing gust. The hair on my head gently sways with the breeze.

"No!" Lily screams.

Hundreds of hands appear beneath me and grab ahold of my legs. They scratch and pull as they try to drag me down. For a moment I feel fingers digging and clawing into my skin. I do not budge. I envision Lily smaller and sporting a baby bonnet. She is now in a cradle that I am rocking back and forth. As I rock the cradle, I sing her a lullaby.

"Rock-a-bye baby, in the treetop When the wind blows, the cradle will rock When the bough breaks, the cradle will fall And down will come baby, cradle and all…"

I see Lily sound asleep in the cradle.

I return to the hallway. Jason is no longer in pain. He is a little dazed and confused. He leans on me.

"Jason, you're going to be OK now," I tell him.

He grins. "Yes, I know…but what just happened?"

"It was a mental attack. The important thing is that you are safe."

We start to walk again. Jason is slow and weak, but I can feel his strength returning with each step. Now I'm impressed by him.

15

I look at Jason, still a little stunned from Lily's attack. Lily will no longer be a problem, but noticing the cameras around us, I realize that we are still far from being able to communicate openly. The only way to talk to him is to do it telepathically. But then again, there might be another way.

I have never brought anybody on a dimensional time trip with me without aid, but I believe I can. I have no choice. I look at Jason and sense agreement. He is ready.

"Close your eyes for a moment," I say. I take a deep breath and then another. I reach out to his mind. It is surprisingly open. I envision a circle of bright energy around his head. This is easier than I imagined.

I hear Jason's voice. "*I am here, Eliza. I have a lot to tell you.*"

I picture a bright yellow tunnel of light, and both of us begin to stream through it. Passing ever so quickly, we move fast, faster than I ever traveled by myself. It must be a combination of our energies. It feels good, actually, like some sort of natural ecstasy rushing through our bodies and minds. I see many doors and openings. I choose a peaceful place. My thoughts direct my reality now. Positive, positive, positive place, I command. The tunnel opens wide, and we are gently dropped onto a meadow. We sit across from each other. I hear the sound of the small waterfall and I smell hibiscus flowers and jasmine. Jason leans over and gives me a gentle hug.

"Eliza, I am so happy you can hear me. I have tried communicating with you for so long. There is a lot to talk about," Jason says.

"For so long? You tried?" I am surprised to hear this, yet at the same time it makes sense. I did feel like Jason was always there for me. So, I am learning, this was not a figment of my imagination.

"No, you weren't imagining my reaching out to you," Jason says. He takes my hand. "They are planning a lot of things that will only harm you and the world."

"I would never cooperate with that."

"You won't have a choice; they are trying to make you a zombie who will blindly work for them," Jason insists.

"How? The same way they did with Cindy to make her so passive.?"

"They are using subtle brainwashing. They are trying to kill your will and kind nature by reinforcing your ego-based reactions. I'm sure they sent Bob after you to see how you would react. They want your emotions to get the better of you."

I shudder. "It has been working, Jason. I start feeling angry, and it takes all my effort to control myself."

"I'm sure they are planning a lot more that I am not aware of. Hell, I wouldn't be surprised if they started drugging you," Jason says.

"What should I do?" I ask.

We both look at each other. The word escape comes in between our minds.

Suddenly, I hear loud noises and a strange ringing sound. I feel nauseous. At that moment, I feel myself being pulled out of my reality with Jason and streaming back through the tunnel. The ringing sounds become louder, as if I have a very angry bee trapped inside my skull.

I open my eyes. Jason and I are back in the hallway. The ringing sound has stopped. We look at each other. We say nothing.

"Jason, tomorrow is a very important mission, I need to get some sleep." I tell him.

Jason puts a hand on my shoulder. "Go to your room and get some rest."

I watch him walk away. My mind is racing again.

16

I toss and turn in my bed, trying to fall asleep again. There have been so many events in the last few days that I feel that I have been pulled into the heart of a tornado. Taking the plane crash trip, saving the baby, Bob attacking me, me striking back, being interrogated, Lily going against me, meeting my mom, discovering the truth about Conners and Cash. And finally, Jason opening up. That was probably the best part of it all. So much in such a short period of time. Maybe it's time for me to escape this place. I am grateful for what I learned here and for how they harnessed my powers and gave me a home—Still, I feel they want to use my powers as tool to get what they want not what's best for me or the world. I can't have that. I'm not their tool!

I could certainly escape with my mind. But my body? That I haven't done yet. I know that I create my realities, that my thoughts and beliefs have power. Could I teleport out of this place?

I want to be able to physically travel through time and space. It's now a matter of belief. I lie back in bed. I take a long deep breath, in and out. I close my eyes and let my mind reach out to the universe. I trust my mind will then show my body how to follow.

I feel myself lifting out of my body. I see my body from up above. I picture the outside of the building in my mind. My astral self is floating upward, through the ceiling. I push through the roof. I float above the building. I send a beam of light into my room through the walls and ceiling and floor, and I see…my body is still there.

I decide to travel with my mind further, just to explore the building and the outside world, which I have never attempted do in the present and with no specific mission or voyagers. But I have nothing to lose now—it is time to push myself farther than I ever have. It is time for me now.

I push harder and try to envision my body—I call it and pull it toward me—and I choose to teleport. I repeat, "Teleport now!" and I see my body begin to rise. I feel relief. But something blocks me from moving beyond the walls. I am sensing silver pulsating waves of energy surround the building. What are these? Some sort of mental dampers? Of course, they already thought this through, they want to prevent us from leaving this place. I am not worried, I believe the dampers are something Jason can help me eliminate. I should go back to my room now and finally get some rest.

"*You cannot leave!*" I hear someone's voice all around me, echoing and resonating within my mind. "*You will die here.*"

I look and see Bob's image floating in front of me. His anger is creating a cloud of gruesome energy. It is nauseating.

"I may be in a coma, but my mind is alive and powerful. You may want to leave or break through these dampers…but I will not allow it!"

I try mentally forcing him back into the building, but his presence is strong. He does not budge.

"You are doomed to stay here in this space, where I am king. You are in my brain now!" he screams. His very words rip into my skin.

Tentacles form out of nowhere. They wrap around me like an angry python, squeezing me, trying to force the life out of me. I cannot move. I can barely think. I need to escape quickly. Bob is laughing at me, taunting me.

17

The mental tentacles Bob has attacked me with coil around me, squeezing harder and harder.

"Bob, what do you want?" I ask him bluntly. I sense his anger, but I still don't understand his motives.

"You are dangerous to this world."

"OK, I have heard that before…what else is new, Bob?"

I feel as if I am talking to the wall. This man is set on one thought: to destroy me. Poor man! Little does he know, I envision him growing into a tiny little dot, imagine his mind becoming nothing.

But that's not what I want. If I do that then I risk becoming what Bob thinks I am—a monster. I need a new way to deal with this, peacefully. I don't want anyone to hurt anymore.

"Jason! Come to me!" I call out with my mind. He doesn't hear me.

"Jason, I need your help!" I imagine myself near him, touching his forehead. "Wake up!"

Jason opens his eyes, and I mentally pull him toward me, right here right now, between me and Bob. He sees that I am surrounded by tentacles. His eyes shoot open.

I hesitate for a moment. "I tried to escape," I tell him. "I tried practicing teleporting…"

"I often suspected that Conners and Cash feared you might try to escape and that they would have something in place to stop you," Jason says slowly.

"They do!" I tell him. "Some sort of mental dampers…but these tentacles are not their doing. It's Bob…"

Bob's giant face appears in front of us. "My body may be beaten, but my mind is stronger than ever. I am going to kill her!" Bob roars. "It is my calling to stop her. To save all…"

"You need to put Bob on ice," Jason says to me. "Do it fast!"

What a wonderful idea.

"You can't stop me from stopping you!" Bob screams. His voice shakes me.

All the while, the tentacles around me are squeezing harder. Yet I do not notice them. I am too busy concentrating, thinking of ice—nice, freezing, soothing ice. The ice surrounds me, protects me. The tentacles trapping me start to turn blue. They freeze solid and become brittle. I shake my body gently. The tentacles shatter into tiny pieces and crumble to the ground like a broken mosaic.

"No!" Bob screams! "It can't be!"

But it can be. I look at Bob's giant head floating in front of me. Putting my hand to my lips, I puff a little breath at him while thinking of ice. My breath fans out and surrounds the image of Bob's head. His head is engulfed in a block of ice. A little chill is good. It has been a hot summer.

"Nooooooo…" Bob's words fade in my brain.

Bob is gone. I am free. I turn to Jason. I kiss him gently on the lips. He looks startled but pleased. I return to my bed, and I am finally out like a light. Deep sleep.

18

After a restful night of sleep, I wake up feeling like a new person. It's been a long time since I got adequate rest. Today is another mission day. I want to do my best, but I also want to leave this place. I just need to find the proper time.

Even though my room is windowless, I can sense the sun starting to rise. Soon Dr. Conners and Mr. Cash will come to prep me and make me travel to the Brighter Day Cult in Wyoming. While I do not like the idea of helping Conners and Cash, letting them profit off my powers, I still want to help. I know this cult is dangerous and needs to be stopped. I could give the FBI the information they need. Perhaps I might even be able to stop the cult. After all, I keep discovering more and more about my abilities. The more challenges I face and overcome, the more my powers grow.

That is what I will do, I decide. I will travel to the cult and see if I can stop them. If nothing else, I will be able to get useful information to the authorities. I know I can do this myself, without being submerged in a sensory deprivation tank. I lie back in my bed, taking a deep breath and then another. Relax, I think to myself, just relax. I picture myself floating up in the morning sky through the air to Wyoming.

Within a moment my astral self is floating above a complex of buildings. A barbed wire fence surrounds the complex. Outside the fence are many police and FBI agents. The agents are nervous, anxious. I can see it in their postures, and I can feel it in their auras.

Looking down on the complex, I see there are three big, white-roofed cement buildings. I have had some training in surveillance. I believe one of the buildings is a dorm, another a storage area, and another a meeting area. This is where the leader, a man who simply goes by the name of Adam, preaches to his followers. I sense that Adam and most of his followers are in the meeting area. I move my astral self to inside the building.

There, standing on a big wooden stage in the middle of the room, is that man, Adam. He is a tall, graying man with green eyes that seem to glow with craziness. I get a chill just looking at him. On the stage next to Adam are four young girls, who are chained and blindfolded. The girls are shivering, crying.

Surrounding the stage, staring intently at Adam, are forty-five people, all dressed in jeans and gray shirts. Out of the forty-five, thirty of them are men. Each of the men is armed with an AK-47, a side arm, and knives. Checking the walls of the building, I find that they are thick concrete. Any assault here would be costly.

I look at Adam on the stage. He is about to speak.

"My followers, my blessed disciples, as you know the way to the divine kingdom is through my word! My word is the word of God. Those outside, those nonbelievers, would lead you to believe their ways are right and ours are wrong! We must show them that our way is the only way. Our way is the gateway to heaven and true ecstasy. I am the sun, the earth, the moon, and the sky. Follow me, and your life will transcend into bliss!"

Adam points dramatically at the girls in chains. "These girls, with their sinful ways, represent all that is bad with the world. We must show them and the rest of the world the right way! We must sacrifice them so the world will learn that our way is right and their way is wrong."

I am disgusted by his words, his actions, his very soul. I have gathered the information I need now—the number of men, how well armed they are, and the location of their fortified position. I can return and give this information to the FBI. But if I do that, and the FBI attacks, these young innocent girls will surely die.

19

I stand there watching Adam lecture his followers at the Brighter Day Cult. Adam has them in the palm of his hand as he rants away.

This crazy man is on a power trip and has a death wish. He is going to bring his followers and these poor innocent girls down with him.

Adam keeps rambling on. "My loving followers, you will help me show them the true way, our way, the one truth." He points dramatically at the poor girls. "We will send out their heads. It will be our statement to the world that we have no fears and will meet all challenges. Yes, we may die, but we will die in a blaze of glory. In that blaze of glory, we will ignite the world with our knowledge."

I am startled by the sight and wonder how could people follow such nonsense. But then again, it is easy to brainwash people. I see Adam's followers are mesmerized, devouring his words blindly. The human psyche fascinates me. Come to think of it, in some ways his followers are just as innocent as the girls on stage.

I just can't stand by and watch these innocents die. How can I prevent this?

"We will follow! We will follow!" the crowd chants in unison.

"No! The things you say are lies!" I say. Since I am in astral form, nobody can actually hear my words. But I hope they can *feel* my words. I send out beams of piercing light-blue energy, trying to awaken them from this oblivion. "Wake up!" I command. "This man is a lie!"

Suddenly the crowd of followers slows its chanting. Their eyes shift from locked on Adam to expressing some doubt.

"You are lying." I say this and picture my words penetrating their minds, becoming their thoughts. "You only care about yourself, your legacy, your ego. You don't care about us."

The expressions on the faces of Adam's followers begin to change. They are all glaring at Adam with contempt. My words are getting through to them. I am amazed and happy at the same time.

One of the people in the front of the crowd points to Adam. "He is a fake!" he shouts. "Let's get him!" says another. They rush the stage.

"What are you doing? Stop! I order you to stop!" Adam pleads, trembling in total shock.

The crowd does not listen to him as they drag him to the ground. They start beating him. The people who had been enthralled by Adam's words are now free from his control. He is finished.

My job here is done. I have proven that I can do good without the assistance of Dr. Conners and Mr. Cash. In fact, I now believe I can do better without them.

I concentrate and envision my pathway back to my room. The tunnel opens up, but it feels different this time, crackling with blue energy, soothing and filling me with unadulterated energy. I feel joy rushing through me. I am streaming through the myriad of colors, and, just as suddenly, I am back in my room, lying in my bed. Wow, what a trip!

I am sure that soon the news will be getting to Dr. Conners and Mr. Cash that the government no longer needs to pay for my services. I am sure they will be angry that they lost high-paying jobs, but I do not care.

I hear a voice inside my mind. It is Cindy. "Eliza, can you hear me?"

I do not respond. After all, these last few days I have learned that my "friends" at the lab, the people who are most like me, cannot be trusted.

"Tom and I know what you did," Cindy thinks to me. "We also know that you and Jason want to leave…"

I am not sure how to respond.

But she continues reaching out to me. "Here's the thing, Eliza. Tom and I are on your side. We have a way to turn off the devices that are keeping you here. Please, Eliza, you have to trust us. Tom and I are not like Lily and Bob. We aren't jealous of you. We don't think you are a danger. We believe you can help the world, and we want to help you and Jason get out of here!"

20

"Trust us," Cindy tells me mentally, as I lie down in my bed. "Tom and I are going to help you get out of this place by taking down the dampers."

I mentally scan their brains, looking for any signs of deception. Their energy fields appear pristine, a light-blue color, which tells me that they are telling the truth.

"Cindy, I appreciate your concern. But whatever I do, I think you should be out of this."

Now I hear Tom's voice in my head. "Eliza, part of the lab's interest in me was that I was an engineer before coming here. I worked on the dampers. Even if you try to get outside somehow, you won't be able to teleport. The dampers actually have a hundred-mile range. That's why when they take you on outside trips, they always stay within that area."

"Oh, that complicates everything," I tell them.

"Eliza, we will help you," Cindy insists. "When you get our signal, teleport away from here freely."

"No, it's too dangerous for you," I stress.

"No, it's too dangerous for everybody else if we do nothing," Tom tells me.

I hear footsteps coming down the hall. I sense it is Dr. Conners, Mr. Cash, Jason, and two guard escorts. Getting up from bed, I realize I am still in my nightgown. I move to my closet quickly and put on my light-blue bodysuit, the one the lab designed for me to use when I do my quantum voyages. I do not want to tip off the others that I already know the cult has been stopped and that my skills will not be needed.

I smile to myself, knowing Conners and Cash have lost their jobs.

There's a knock on the door.

I walk over and open the door. I enter the hallway. "I have done the mental preparation for my voyage," I say, very matter of fact.

Dr. Conners and Mr. Cash both look upset, though they are trying to mask their feelings with fake smiles.

Dr. Conners puts a hand on my shoulder. "Apparently, our services are no longer needed by the FBI," he tells me.

I look him in the eyes to see if he will offer up any other information. He meets my glance with stone-cold silence.

"It seems like the cult rallied against their leader and killed him," Jason says, breaking the silence. "All the hostages are safe. There were no other casualties."

"That is great news," I say with a smile. I keep my eyes on Dr. Conners and Mr. Cash. Their bodies are slumped. They are truly not happy with this result. "Since we have some free time now, I would love to go on a road trip," I mention. "I am exhausted with the last week of events and want to be mentally ready for the next missions," I say. I hesitate for a moment and then add, "I've always wanted to go to Yosemite."

Dr. Conners and Mr. Cash exchange quick glances.

"Ah, that's quite the road trip," Dr. Conners says with a weak smile. "A trip like that is possible, but it takes a lot of planning. We can arrange something closer though. At Golden Gate Park, for example, you would get your recharge and relaxation."

Yeah, I can see Cindy and Tom are right. Conners and Cash don't want me traveling past the dampers' area.

Right at that moment, I hear Cindy's words in my mind. "Eliza, we are ready. When you hear our signal, teleport away from here." A slight pause then Cindy adds, "I won't let them do to you what that have done to me. Good thing they don't have as much control as they believe!

I don't know what they are up to, but I sense that Cindy and Tom are going to sacrifice themselves for me. I cannot let them do this. I cannot take any of this any longer. I take a quick deep breath, then another. I picture in my mind everything around me moving slower and slower until it eventually stops.

"Eliza, what's wrong with…" Jason starts to say, until he and everybody around him freeze in place.

Touching Jason on the shoulder, I tell him, "Come on, Jason; we're getting out of here."

Jason unfreezes and finishes his statement, "…you?"

He looks around at the frozen Dr. Conners, Mr. Cash, and the guards. "Eliza, what did you do?"

I take him by the hand and start pulling him down the hall. "I slowed time to a near stop so we can get out of here," I say frantically. "I do not know how long I can hold it."

Jason follows my lead, and we both start racing down the hallway.

"We have to get out of here fast and as far away as possible," I say, running. "Do you know of any place far away from here where we would be safe?"

Jason is now running a little ahead of me, actually pulling me a bit through the maze of hallways. "Yes, my family has a cabin in Maine that nobody knows about."

"Good," I say as we continue racing through the hallways. "Just picture it in your mind. When we get far enough away from here, I will take us there."

We reach the main door that leads to the outside. We push through the door. The sun hits us in the face. With time slowed like this, it somehow does not seem as warm and as comforting as I think it should. That is the least of my worries now, though.

"But Eliza, the range on the dampers has to be miles," Jason says.

I pull Jason around the corner of the main building, toward the parking lot.

"That's why we will take a car and drive until we get out of range," I tell Jason.

"Do you know how to hotwire a car? 'Cause I sure don't," he says.

"No, but that will not be necessary. We will just borrow a car that is already started but time frozen."

"Ah, good point," Jason says.

I spot the perfect car for us. It is a red hatchback, driven by a short man with glasses. The driver was just pulling into the parking lot through the security gate as I slowed time.

"Come on, hurry," I tell Jason. "The gate to the facility is frozen open. This is our chance..."

As we get about ten feet from the car, I imagine time starting to move again. The once-frozen world springs back to life. I pull Jason toward the car.

The driver sees us. He looks confused but not worried. The guards at the gate see us, too. They will react to us soon enough.

Alarms start going off all over the complex.

"Oh, this is bad," Jason says.

"Halt!" one of the guards shouts, holding his hand out straight.

I try to mentally sedate him by sending the command "Sleep!" in my mind as I look at him. But it doesn't work. The time-stop has taken too much out of me.

"This is for you, Eliza," I hear Cindy and Tom say in my mind.

An explosion rocks the compound. The force from the explosion jolts us all.

"What the heck was that?" Jason asks.

"That's our chance," I say, leaning into Jason. "Think of the cabin now."

"Stop them! Stop them!" I hear Mr. Cash shouting. "Guards, use deadly force!"

"Wait, no! We don't want them killed!" Conners cries.

Too late. A bullet rings out.

I repeat to Jason, "Think of the cabin now. Look at me and project the image to me! Do it quickly." Jason takes a breath, staring at me. I see a beautiful small cabin near a lake. I paint it in bright colors. I hear the wind, and picture us both standing there now. I want to be there now. We stream though the whirlpool of cosmic meanderings…The wind is blowing, playing with my hair. I smell nature, so sweet and soothing. I am surrounded by trees. I see an old cabin on my right.

"We did it!" Jason says, hugging me. "We did it."

I kiss Jason finally. What a sweet, long-awaited kiss.

We are safe. But at what cost? I am afraid. Cindy and Tom died for our freedom. I also know that Mr. Cash and Dr. Conners will stop at nothing to get me back, but that is not going to happen. I am now free and I am determined to stay this way.

21

I wake up in my bed with Jason next to me. I kiss him gently on his left cheek and give him a few more little kisses. He smiles. I feel so happy now. I dreamt of this moment for so long. Part of me is very happy to be here with Jason, but part of me is concerned with the unknown. Jason gets up to make some coffee. I look out the window, taking in the surrounding woods; it looks so serene, just like the places I used to envision in my mind during personal escapes while in the lab. Jason comes back holding a cup.

"There is no coffee, but I have some herbal tea for you," Jason says. "How are you feeling?"

Sitting up in bed, I take a sip of the tea. "I'm tired, relieved, sad, and happy all at the same time," I sigh.

Jason sits down beside me.

I turn away, gazing out the window. "Cindy and Tom were killed in the explosion, along with two guards."

Putting his hand gently on my shoulder, Jason comforts me. "You shouldn't feel guilty, Eliza. This is what Cindy and Tom wanted for you—to be free and out of the clutches of Conners and Cash."

Looking Jason in the eyes, I ask, "But was it worth the cost of their lives?"

"What happened happened," he says. "It's past now. We need to focus on the here and now and the rest of our lives."

I shake my head. "The lab still exists. They can find more special people and abuse their powers. Hell, Jason, I'm sure they will come looking for me."

Jason smiles. I can't help but feel a little better. He leans in and kisses me. "Eliza, we're off the grid here. They can't find us right now…there is no Internet, no TV, nothing." He pauses for a moment. "Maybe later on, when things calm down, we will try to get close to civilization."

Jason bends over and kisses me. "I'll to go to the local store get us some coffee and food. Do you want to come?" he asks. "It's beautiful out."

"I just need a little more rest."

Jason stands up and smiles. "I'll be back in a flash."

When Jason gets back, I am sitting at the kitchen table, looking out the window at the lush forest that surrounds us. I'm starting to feel a little more secure here. Nature always soothes me. I take a deep breath and relax a bit. That is, until I see Jason's face. He is pale as a ghost.

"Jason, what's wrong?"

Jason shakes his head and drops a newspaper down onto the table. He opens the paper up and there are our pictures on page two under a caption reading, "Suspected Terrorists in Lab Bombing."

"I can't believe Cash and Conners are blaming the explosion at the lab on us," I moan. "Now every police officer and sheriff or deputy in the country will be looking for us."

Jason shakes his head. "Perhaps, but I don't think anybody recognized me at the corner store. After all, nobody thinks two terrorists who blew up a lab in California would be here."

I look up at Jason. "Still, we can't be sure of that. I don't want to spend the rest of our lives hiding and on the run."

Jason shakes his head. "This isn't what I signed up for. Back when Dr. Conners first recruited me, he seemed so sincere. Like he wanted to make the world a better place by exploring the human mind and all it could do…I just don't know what happened to him."

"Mr. Cash happened to him," I tell Jason. "That man only cares about profit, and he got to Dr. Conners…He has slowly brainwashed him."

Suddenly, Jason's eyes shoot open. "Then we—well, you—have to stop him from meeting Cash."

I shake my head. "Jason, I wish I could, but I can't travel back that far in time. I can only jump to nearby times. I certainly can't jump back to before I was born."

"No, no, no!" Jason says, taking my hand. "I am confident you can. The only reason you can't is that you think you can't. It's your belief that stops you, you know that."

"Yes, I know, Jason, but sometimes the problem with a limiting belief is that it is so intrinsic that it is almost impossible to overcome. It is so deeply engrained in me. I know I can convince myself of the opposite— that yes, I can travel back way back in time—but it can only last for so long. Then the negative old belief comes back and throws everything offf."

"What if I guide you back in time? I will use my voice, instead of you trying to convince yourself mentally. I will keep giving you positive mental reinforcement for as long as you are gone," Jason says. He takes me by the hand, smiles, and looks me in the eyes. "You trust me, don't you?"

"Of course I do, Jason."

"Great! Then let's do this!"

We move into the living room. We sit on the couch. I close my eyes and naturally drift off.

I feel myself slowly lifting up now. I breathe deeply and lift yet higher. I see Jason next to me from up above. He is speaking slowly to me.

"You are easily traveling back in time, back to before you were born. You can, you always have, and you can stay there for as long as you need to," Jason says, sitting next to me. I hear these positive words, and I take them with me as I travel back in time. Back to before I was born. I can do it. Yes, easily and effortlessly. I believe I can; I have no doubt. Suddenly, a tunnel opens up, and I am streaming very quickly. Swirling matter, colorful energies, all penetrating through me. It feels refreshing. I feel confident I am going in the right direction. I want to meet Conners before he met Cash.

22

I open my eyes, and I am standing outside in an open green area. There are brick buildings all around me. People, young people, are going in and out of the buildings. Some are serious. Others are laughing. Almost all of them are carrying books. I'm on a college campus. I'm just not sure where or, for that matter, when.

Studying a few of the passing students, I notice that none of them are talking on cell phones. In fact, I see no wireless devices or tablets. There are a couple of students sitting on the grass, looking at a white, boxy portable computer. They seem very excited about this—like it is a new experience.

I think about approaching one of the students and asking him what the date is and where I am. But I realize if I did that he would think I'm crazy or drugged out. The last thing I need now is to draw attention to myself. As near as I can tell, though, from the lack of cell phones and the overall fashion sense of the student population, I'm in the late 1980s.

I notice a few of the students are wearing UMass T-shirts—Massachusetts University, where Dr. Conners started his studies. I had traveled back through time to the place I needed to be. Now I just need to find the right building.

I stop a male student passing by. "Excuse me. Can you help me?" I ask with a smile. "I seem to be lost. I don't come to this part of the campus that often."

The student returns my smile. "How can I help you?"

"I'm looking for the neurosciences department," I say, shyly.

He points to a tall redbrick building at the end of the quad. "I'm pretty sure it's that one."

"Thanks," I tell him as I head toward the building.

Walking up the cold, white cement stairs into the neurosciences building, I'm both nervous and excited. There's a staff directory on the wall next to the entrance. A quick glance shows that Dr. Jeffery Conners has an office and lab on the second floor, room 222. I take a deep breath and head down the hall to a staircase.

While climbing up the stairs to the second floor, my mind races with possibilities. I am not sure what to tell him. What will he believe? Can I even trust him? How can I convince him that I'm who I say I am?

The second floor is a long shiny corridor. I walk past room after room, checking the numbers: 200, 202, 204. My heart starts racing with anticipation, beating faster as the numbers grow. The faster my heart beats, the slower my feet move. I should be excited. I am excited. But I am also worried. What if I fail? Then all is lost, both in the past and the future. I shake my head. I can't think that way. I won't think that way. Like they say, failure is not an option.

It must be obvious that I am lost in my thoughts as a slightly familiar voice calls out to me.

"Excuse me, miss—if you are here to be a part of the precognition study, you've gone too far."

Stopping and turning toward the voice, I notice I had just walked right past room 222. Walking back toward the room, I smile. "Sorry, a lot on my mind," I explain.

There, sitting at a big desk in the middle of the room, is Dr. Conners. He has more hair than I am used to, and that hair is much darker. He is also trimmer than the man I know. But it is still him.

Dr. Conners points to a chair across from his desk. "Please come in and sit down. I generally ask students some preliminary questions to see if they qualify for the study." He looks at me with a curious eye. "Are you are a graduate student?" he asks.

"Yes," I tell him as I settle into the chair.

He grins. "Funny. I've never seen you around. Yet you look so familiar…"

"I'm getting my master's in fine arts," I say, hoping this covers me. I shrug. "I guess I just have one of those faces."

"Do you have your student ID card with you?" Dr. Conners asks. "I need that to register you for the study."

I pause. "Before I give you that, I have some questions for you," I tell him.

He leans into the desk and smiles. "I love questions."

"What's the goal of this study?" I ask.

He sits back in his chair. "Well, the goal of this particular study is to find what parts of the brain are most active during precognition." He takes a second to think a little more. "My overall goal is to unlock certain mental capabilities of the mind. With the tools available today, I can make progress my predecessors could only dream of."

"Oh, how so?" I prompt.

His smile broadens and his eyes fill with life. "This is 1985. We have MRIs that give us exact pictures of the brain. Plus, we've just put in a grant for a new PET scanner. The possibilities that open up are endless." He looks me in the eyes. "I'm very excited about our research here. We are doing state-of-the-art work. Any other questions?"

OK, so, I traveled a bit farther back than planned. Still, I can use this to my advantage. I hesitate for a moment and then ask bluntly, "Where do you get your funding?"

"Excuse me?"

"Where does your funding come from?" I repeat.

"That's a strange kind of question coming from a research study candidate. What does it matter to you?"

I hesitate again, but then decide to lay it all on the line. "I'm concerned because I am one of your test subjects," I say quickly.

Dr. Conners looks at me, eyes wide open. "Not yet, young lady. I need to do some testing first and see if you qualify." He smiles at me.

"I know this may sound crazy, but I won't be born for another five years, and you won't meet me until about ten years after that."

Dr. Conners looks at me with caution. He thinks I am crazy. I can see it in his face. He lifts the phone and presses a button. "Hello, security. I have an intruder in Room 222."

I reach out and touch Dr. Conners gently on the hand. Pleading with my eyes, I say, "You have to believe me. Soon you will be approached by Raymond Cash."

"The billionaire?"

"Yes."

He laughs. "Yeah, the billionaire is going to come to me. Billionaires are always coming to me, begging for me to take their money." He stops to collect his thoughts. "Billionaires and investment bankers all want a quick return for their investments. My research is long term."

"Raymond Cash understands that. He sees the potential in your work," I tell Dr. Conners.

"My work does have great potential," he says.

"Yes, and I know you want to use your work for good. But Cash will have other plans. He wants to use your work for ulterior motives. If you go with him, your research and study will go awry. This alliance won't do any good for the world." I look down.

Dr. Conners just stares at me with a raised eyebrow.

He reaches into his desk and pulls out a deck of cards. "Let's give you a simple test," he says pulling a card off the top of the deck. Looking at the card, he asks me, "I'm picturing this card in my mind now. Can you tell me which card this is?"

I should be able to do this. I clear my mind while concentrating on the card. Sadly, for some reason, I can't see the card. I take a deep breath and then another. Yet my mind draws a blank. The time travel is exhausting. I feel the old belief—that I can't be here—creeping in. It makes me dizzy. I try to find a signal where Jason's words can be heard. I tune in. I can be here. I am capable of this. But still, I have a hard time seeing the card. My mind is busy with conflicting thoughts. I breathe in deeply.

"This should be easy for me," I tell Dr. Conners.

"It is a fairly basic test," he answers. "Can you even tell me the suit?"

I know I have a one in four chance of guessing, yet I don't want to guess. I want to see the card in my mind. I refuse to guess. "It's unclear to me," I sputter. "I think the time travel wore me out."

Dr. Conners shakes his head. "I'm sorry, miss. I just don't believe you."

Two security guards dressed in brown uniforms appear behind me in the doorway.

"You called for us, Dr. Conners?" one of the security guards, a large man with a beard, asks.

"Yes. Yes, I did," Dr. Conners says. "Can you please escort this woman out of my office and off campus?"

"Of course," the large security guard obeys. The two guards walk up to me and put their hands on my shoulders. "Come with us please, ma'am."

Now is the time for me to show Dr. Conners what I can really do. I may not be able to demonstrate my time-travel powers, and my mind reading didn't work, but putting thoughts and suggestions into people's minds—that's something that comes fairly naturally to me. I need to be able to do this in order to prove to Dr. Conners that I am not, as Bob would say, a loon.

"*There is no need to take me away*," I tell the guards. "*Dr. Conners and I are just chatting nicely.*"

The guards pull me up off the chair. "Sorry, lady, we work for the University, not you," the second guard, a skinny man with beady eyes, tells me.

The two guards start pulling me away from Dr. Conners, toward the door. I try to resist, but they are too strong and for some reason my powers aren't working. It has to be my nerves. I need to calm down and believe in myself.

"Do you want to press charges, Dr. Conners?" one of the security guards questions.

Dr. Conners just shakes his head. "No, she's mostly harmless," he tells the guards. Looking at me, he adds, "Please get help, young lady."

"My name is Eliza, Eliza Tuman," I tell him.

"Well, Ms. Tuman, please get help," I hear Dr. Conners repeat, as the guards drag me out of the room.

While the guards lead me out of the building into the quad, I work on calming my mind and my body.

"Listen," I say to the guards. "You don't have to escort me off campus. I know when I'm not wanted…"

"Our orders are our orders," the larger guard tells me coldly, continuing to lead me away from the building. "We don't listen to people we are escorting off campus."

"You're lucky the professor doesn't want to press charges," the other one says.

We walk for a few minutes in silence. I need to get back to Dr. Conners and convince him I am what I say I am and that he must avoid Mr. Cash. As we walk, I try to muster my energy and focus my concentration. I look at the guards and try to envision their brains. I focus on the part of their brains that produces melatonin. I see it now, and it is releasing more and more in the brains of both of them, more melatonin to relax them, and naturally sedate them. The more I envision this, the more relaxed they feel, walking slower. One is yawning. They both look drowsy and comfortably relaxed. That's right. This is all I need. They will now be more receptive to me and my every word.

I look at them, and slowly say, "You let me go now. I am safe. I am just another student. You simply go about your business now, and you will ignore any calls from Conners for the next few hours."

The two guards nod to me and walk away slowly.

I turn and head back toward Dr. Conners's office.

When I reach him, he is sitting in his office, staring at a computer screen. Somehow, he seems to sense me at the door, and he looks up as I walk into the office.

"Well, Ms. Tuman, you are nothing if not persistent."

"My cause is an important one," I tell him.

"Interestingly enough, your name did ring a bell. I looked it up in my database. One of my test subjects is a Tuman…"

"Yes, Stewart Tuman is my father."

I think, finally, I am getting his attention.

"You have to understand why I do find this hard to believe. You are a few years older than the man you claim is your father."

"Do you have his DNA on file? You can take some of mine to prove I am his daughter."

Dr. Conners shakes his head. "It's 1985. The technology to do what you want is very rare and very expensive."

Dr. Conners picks up the phone.

"Security won't respond to your call," I tell him.

Dr. Conners starts to fidget anxiously at his desk. He has a right to be nervous. After all, I do sound kind of crazy. I need to do something to prove to him that I am what I claim to be. I close my eyes and take a few deep breaths. I figure the best way to show him what I can do is to perform a quick time-stop. But I don't want to chance leaving this time period yet, so I try holding time still for just a moment. I take a deep breath and think to myself—"slow." I repeat the word with each breath. The world blurs and then comes to a halt. I move to Dr. Conners's desk, take pen and paper, and write a note. I turn the paper over. I return to my original spot in the office. With another deep breath, I concentrate on everything moving again. A flash of light and a rush of energy go right through me.

Pointing to the piece of paper on the desk, I tell Dr. Conners, "I left you a note just now."

"But that's impossible; you haven't moved," he declares, picking up the piece of paper. He looks at it, and reads the note out loud. "Dr. Conners, please trust me." He smiles. "OK, you have my attention now."

Dr. Conners gets up quickly and shuts the door to his office. He sits on the top of his desk and looks at me.

"I really want to believe what you are telling me. But surely you understand how far-fetched it sounds."

Leaning against the wall, I answer, "But why would I make any of this up? What could I possibly have to gain by asking you simply to avoid Mr. Cash when he calls?" I look him squarely in the eyes. "Dr. Conners, you are at the precipice now, where you'll be able to help humans make great strides. I know your intentions are noble, but if you take Mr. Cash's money, your ideals will be corrupted. People will be hurt."

"They do say money can corrupt," he admits. He smiles and then adds, "Though I would love the chance to test that."

"No, you wouldn't," I insist.

Dr. Conners looks up at the ceiling and sighs. "Here's the deal, though," he explains, looking back at me. "Research isn't cheap. I'm going to need funding. Which I am sure I will get. But I need serious funding if I want to set up a facility at some point. Research grants and government assistance won't help enough. I need a private investor."

"I've been thinking about how I can help." I pause for a moment. "After all, I do know certain things about the future...things that you can use to your advantage. For instance, I know you're a baseball fan and a Mets fan. Well, the Mets are going to win the World Series next year."

"Well, that prediction is not too far-fetched," Dr. Conners admits. "After all, they are having a good year this year."

***

"They don't just win; they win one hundred and sixteen games."

***

"I hope you're right," Dr. Conners says.

"You should buy Apple stock now."

He smiles. "Apple, the ones who make that cute little computer? They survive?"

"They not only survive; they flourish."

He looks at me confused. "Are you sure? I hear their founder Steven Jobs just left the company. Their stock is in disarray."

"Perfect! Buy as much as you can now. It will be worth over five hundred dollars a share in my time and then split seven for one..."

"Wow..."

"Around 1994, the World Wide Web will appear. Soon after that, every company will want to have a presence there. Buy up all the web addresses you can, like IBM.com, ABC.com—you get the idea. Plus, there are going to be certain companies that take off when the Internet booms.

Some pertinent names are Yahoo, Amazon, Google, and Facebook. These will be good investments."

As I talk, Dr. Conners starts jotting down notes on the piece of paper with my note. "You will be able to use your Apple stock money to get in on the ground floor with these companies. Amazon is founded by a man named Jeff Bezos, Yahoo by Jerry Yang, Google by Larry Page, and Facebook by Mark Zuckerberg while he was still at Harvard."

"I see you have an eidetic memory," Dr. Conners observes.

I smile. "Actually, I had no idea that I did until just now."

Suddenly I feel dizzy and weak, and everything around me starts to blur and swirl together. I am losing my grip on this time. Something is pulling me out. I feel that my time here has come to a close. It is becoming harder and harder to stay.

"I don't have much time left in this time," I say, touching Dr. Conners on the hand. "Please use all the information I gave you wisely, and remember to avoid Mr. Cash. See you in the future!" I am pulled out, streaming all the way forward in time, back to my present where I left off. I feel relief and success. Now I just want to wake up near Jason.

23

I open my eyes and find myself standing outside of Jason's cabin. Strangely, I landed in a different location. I guess reality has been modified, or else I time-walked a bit. I feel drained, yet anxious.

I bound up the stairs to the cabin, my heart pounding with excitement. I hear Jason's voice through the door. He is chatting with someone.

I stop and peer into the window. Jason is standing in the living room, holding the hand of a young blond woman. The way he looks at her is the way he looked at me when we were here. She looks unsure, sad. I am not sure who she is. The future did change. This is a new timeline. It means that Conners made something different. I look at Jason and this woman, and I feel lost. Jason's path and mine are separate here. I see the woman's eyes. It is what it is I think. I turn away.

I sense a wave signal, a familiar frequency; someone is trying to contact me. I open up to signal.

"Eliza, where are you?" I hear in my mind. I try to tune more to the wave, where the voice is coming from.

"Cindy...it's you..." I think to her.

"Of course it's me, silly; who else sends you mental status reports?"

I back away from the porch. Yes, in this future, I was no longer with Jason, but Cindy was alive. My time travel had done some good.

"Oh, your mom also called to remind you that you are doing dinner with them next week. She says she knows you have a photographic memory, but she still likes to remind you," Cindy thinks to me.

Oh my God, my parents are still alive in this time. I may have lost Jason, but my travel has done so much good.

"Now, come on, boss; get back to the lab," Cindy coaxes in my mind. *"You have an executive meeting with Dr. C in like ten minutes. Where are you, anyhow?"*

"Maine."

"Man, I wish I could teleport like you. You have all the coolest powers…"

I close my eyes and concentrate on returning to my room at the lab. I feel a rush of energy engulfing me. My entire body tingles and then stops, and I open my eyes. I'm in a room, but it's different than my room as I remember it. This one is big and spacious and filled with personal mementos. I look at the pictures on the nightstand. They are photos of my parents and me throughout the years. I hear a knock on a door coming from another room. Walking out of the bedroom, I enter a living area far nicer than before, much more plush and comfy. I even have windows looking out into the world.

I open the door and Dr. Conners is standing there, smiling.

"Dr. Conners," I begin.

He smiles. "Doctor? Why so formal. You haven't called me doctor in nearly ten years." His eyes pop open. He walks into my room and shuts the door behind him. "So this is the day? The day you went back in time and started all this."

We sit down on my couch. "Yes, I'm still a little stunned by everything. I was so happy when I heard Cindy in my mind."

"So things are that much different than the original timeline?"

"Yes, Cindy was killed…"

"Well, she's very much alive here. In fact, she and Tom are expecting their second child."

"Wow, what about Lily and Bob? Are they here?"

Dr. Conners gives me a nod. "Yes, they are senior instructors. Much to the chagrin of many of our students."

I sigh. "It's funny; I instigated all these changes, but I can't remember any of them."

Dr. Conners touches me gently on the shoulder. "Yes, we always knew this might happen. Like I say, time travel is wacky."

I give him a small smile. "Is that your scientific explanation, Doctor?"

"Your power is incredible, Eliza. In our twenty years together, I've still never seen anybody even close to you. Yet even your power has its limits and costs. In this case, doing what you did, going back in time to change things, cost you your memory of what happened. Your last twenty years have been quite different in this reality."

"I'm just glad you believed me."

"When you disappeared right before my eyes but I still had a hand-written message from you, I had no choice but to believe you. I'm so glad I did. I know you've lost your past now, but believe me you've gained so much more."

I look away. "My past isn't my only loss."

"Oh?"

"There was a man who helped me a lot in that old reality. We became very close. But I saw him in this reality and he was with someone else..."

"I'm so sorry, Eliza, but I swear to you what we have accomplished here is amazing. And there are plenty of fish in the sea..."

I know he is correct. I am happy that the facility is in the right hands and that so many people are alive.

Dr. Conners stands up. "Tomorrow, I will show you the facility and all we've accomplished. I also am greatly interested in learning how different this reality is from the one you remember. For today, though, just take it easy and rest. There's certainly nothing pressing for you to do."

Dr. Conners—well, Mark—heads to the door. He stops and turns to me. "Oh, tomorrow we will be interviewing new research associate candidates. Look at some résumés on your table. You need a colleague, someone who can help you get caught up fast. One of the candidates is especially interesting. Not only does he have a PhD in biopsychology, but he has an MBA as well."

Conners smiles and leaves.

I look down at the résumés and see one for the candidate Dr. Conners mentioned. Indeed, it is an impressive résumé. I look at his name. It says Jason Bray. I smile more.

www.ingramcontent.com/pod-product-compliance
Lightning Source LLC
Chambersburg PA
CBHW071344130626

46556CB00005B/2027